Y0-CBA-747

It's Summer, Dear Dragon

by Margaret Hillert
Illustrated by David Schimmell

NORWOOD HOUSE PRESS

The **Dear Dragon** series is comprised of carefully written books that extend the collection of classic readers you may remember from your own childhood. Each book features text focused on common sight words. Through the use of controlled text, these books provide young children with abundant practice recognizing the words that appear most frequently in written text. Rapid recognition of high-frequency words is one of the keys for developing automaticity which, in turn, promotes accuracy and rate necessary for fluent reading. The many additional details in the pictures enhance the story and offer opportunities for students to expand oral language and develop comprehension.

Shannon Cannon

Shannon K. Cannon, Ph.D.
Literacy Consultant

Norwood House Press • P.O. Box 316598 • Chicago, Illinois 60631
For more information about Norwood House Press please visit our website at
www.norwoodhousepress.com or call 866-565-2900.

Text copyright ©2010 by Margaret Hillert. Illustrations and cover design
copyright ©2010 by Norwood House Press, Inc. All rights reserved. No part of
this book may be reproduced or utilized in any form or by any means without
written permission from the publisher.

Paperback ISBN: 978-1-60357-093-0

The Library of Congress has cataloged the original hardcover edition with the
following call number: 2009003889

277R–022015
Manufactured in the United States of America in North Mankato, Minnesota.

Come here. Come here.
Come to my house.
I will do this and we can have fun.

Oh. Oh.
My mother wants me.
I will come back.

What, Mother?
Do you want me to help?
I can work, work, work.

Yes, yes.
Put all of this away.
Then you can go back there.

Get in. Get in.
Now we can play.
This is good.

I will put this on here.
Then we can eat.
It will be fun.

Here comes Father.

Come on.
Come on.
See what Mother did.
It looks good, good, good.

Oh, boy.
Do you see what I see?
Can we go now?

It looks so good!
Here is one for me—
and one for you.

Come now.
Put this on.
We have to go.

Yes.
I want to go.
I like to play.

Away we go.
Away, away, away.

Here we are.
This is the spot.
I see my friends.

Now I will do this.
One, two, three!
There it goes!

Did you see me, Father?
Did you see me?

Yes. Yes.
You were good.

Now we have to go.
We will go away, away, away.
We will see something good.

What was that?
Did you see that?

Look, look.
Oh, oh, oohhh!

Here you are with me.
And here I am with you.
What fun. What fun, dear dragon.

WORD LIST

It's Summer, Dear Dragon **uses the 65 words listed below.**
This list can be used to practice reading the words that appear in the text.
You may wish to write the words on index cards and use them to help your
child build automatic word recognition. Regular practice with these words
will enhance your child's fluency in reading connected text.

all	Father	like	that
am	for	look(s)	the
and	friends		then
are	fun	me	there
away		Mother	this
	get	my	three
back	go		to
be	goes	now	two
boy	good		
		of	want(s)
can	have	oh	was
come(s)	help	on	we
	here	one	were
dear	house		what
did		play	will
do	I	put	with
dragon	in		work
	is	see	
eat	it	so	yes
		something	you
		spot	

ABOUT THE AUTHOR

Margaret Hillert has written over 80 books for children who are just learning to read. Her books have been translated into many different languages and over a million children throughout the world have read her books. She first started writing poetry as a child and has continued to write for children and adults throughout her life. A first grade teacher for 34 years, Margaret is now retired from teaching and lives in Michigan where she likes to write, take walks in the morning, and care for her three cats.

Photograph by Glenna Washburn

ABOUT THE ADVISOR

Shannon K. Cannon is a teacher educator, staff developer, and curriculum writer. She earned her doctorate in Language, Literacy, and Culture from the University of California Davis, where she serves on their clinical faculty supervising pre-service teachers, teaching elementary methods courses in reading/language arts and technology, and teaching Master's courses in inquiry. She began her career teaching second grade. She then spent over 15 years in educational publishing where her work included developing and writing curricular programs as well as providing professional development support to classroom teachers.

ABOUT THE ILLUSTRATOR

David Schimmell served as a professional firefighter for 23 years before hanging up his boots and helmet to devote himself to working as an illustrator of children's books. David has happily created illustrations for the New Dear Dragon books as well as the artwork for educational and retail book projects. Born and raised in Evansville, Indiana, he lives there today with his wife and family.